Revenge at Shepherds Pass

Alex Mitchell

Published by Alex Mitchell, 2023.

REVENGE AT SHEPHERDS PASS

First edition. October 9, 2023.

Copyright © 2023 Alex Mitchell.

ISBN: 979-8891980044

Written by Alex Mitchell.

Also by Alex Mitchell

Revenge at Shepherds Pass
Welcome to Shepherds Pass

Chapter 1

The US Marshals Service is the oldest law enforcement agency in the United States, having been put into place by George Washington and the First US Congress. It has duties have been modified over the years, but the foundation has remained primarily intact.

On and unseasonably warm fall evening a bus operated by the US Marshals service left the Jefferson City Missouri Federal Courts building bound for Chillicothe women's prison in upstate Missouri. The bus had ten female passengers and three marshals supervising the prisoner return. The old blue due to be retired soon. Marshals bus drove highway 70 first without incidence. As is common in Missouri in the fall even fell quickly and the dark begun to threaten the light. The driver noticed smoke rising from the highway in front of him and lights flashing signaling the highway patrol and possible the fire department.

"Looks like a car fire ahead. Signal the house we are going to be late." The drive commanded one of the guards. It is standard protocol that any deviation from their assigned plan had to be noted and called in to command. After buzzing static and a bad connection the second Mashal confirmed they were free to follow the detour that was being advertised by the highway crew. There was a gowning from the passengers. Usually, any deviation from the daily routine of prisoners is seen as a cause to celebrate however they were sure the delay meant they might miss supper have to wait for day to eat. "Pipe down ladies we are going to miss the same meal you are." The third marshal reassured the prisoners.

The traffic thinned out and there was space between the vehicles, and they wound slowly down an outer road clearly not meant for high-speed traffic. Suddenly there was a flash and a huge boom. The front of windshield of the bus was bullet resistant glass and it shatter. "Oh Shit." The driver yelled. In an instant he knew what was happening. They were under attack. There is no such thing as bullet proof glass, only bullet resistant glass. The first shot to the window must have come from an extremely heavy caliber weapon he thought for it shattered the window. "We're under attack." The drive yelled. The other two marshals stared reaching for their side arms in between prayers. One more 50. Caliber round and the drives window would be compromised, and it would shatter into a polycarbonate dust. It happened almost in a second. The second 50. Caliber round dropped the front windshield and caused the drivers head to explode as the round continued it destructive path. There was screaming from the prisoners as the bus swerved. Any side traffic speeded up and gave the bus a clear path to its demises. The Second Marshal reached over the soup that was now the driver to steer the bus. He knew there was no way to get control of the pedals, so his best bet was to aim the bus for a ditch and hope for the best. The bus hit the ditch and slide on his side. The second marshal climbed out of the door to the bus. His body armor light up and burst as the 50. Caliber round shot through it as if he were wearing a cheap tee shirt. Two large men walked slowly toward the bus. They both had hunting rifles. The third marshal had been knocked unconscious by the crash. The two men pulled the third marshal from the bus and dropped him on the side of the road. "Where is the key to the back and the cuffs?" The first of the large men commanded. The marshal looked at the men as if he was considering his options, as if he had any. The large man smacked the marshal in the face with the butt of the riffle and before the second strike the marshal presented the key. "Thank you." The large man said just before shooting the marshal in the head.

"All right ladies everyone lines up." The second of the large men instructed as they released the women prisoners from the back of the bus. Women prisoner number ten was Julia Poole. Julia Poole rushed to the two men and hugged them. The first of the large men walked over to Willow Rushmore one of the prisoners and handed her some money. "You run in that direction." He commanded.

"What?" Willow seemed totally confused.

"Excuse me sir one of the other women in line." Interrupted. The man looked at the woman interrupting as if his patience was being tested.

"Give me my money and I'm out of here. She aint too bright and time is wasting."

"You understand what we are doing don't you."

"Yelp."

"Why don't you explain it to the class."

"You are going to give us all money and send us in different direction to confuse the hunting dogs they are will be sending."

"You get an A." He handed her money and pointed where she was to run, and she was off without another word. The other women except Julia Poole all excepted their money and was off. Julia stripped off her clothes and handed them to one of the other women the then rubbed herself in a mix that had been brought by the two large men. She then slipped on a jumpsuit from a plastic bag. The mixture she rubbed herself in was made of wild onion. Something found all over the woods. The trio set fire to the marshal's bus then took off.

Chapter 2

"It is way too early in the morning for whatever this is we are doing." Detective Don Nash complained. The detectives, the sergeants and their partners has been called for an early morning meeting. Shepherds Pass has a new police station, and they were taking advantage of one of the conference rooms at five o'clock in the morning. All the police that had been requested gave their individual disapproval for the early meeting.

"Sorry for the early start guys but we have guest, and we are on their timetable." Lt. Dana Crawford comment to her unit, even though she knew it would not stop the growing.

Detective Lavon Tyler entered the room with his partner Abby Blackwell. Abby saw one of the female patrolmen, Webber and the women exchanged angry glances. Webber was the partner of Wendell Bishop. Bishop has just been assigned as a Sargent. He and Lavon had become fast friends since Lavon's recent arrival to Shepherds Pass.

"If you don't stop giving her the evil eye, I am going to start a rumor that the two of you are lovers and may have just had a bad break up." Lavon whispered to Abby.

"You can be such an asshole when you want to be." She whispered back. But she broke off the staring contest.

"Alright ladies and gentlemen I give you the US Marshals Service. Marshal Andrew Tobias please take over." Coleman announced and the room went totally silent Marshal Tobias and at all man in his fifties. He was physically fit with a box haircut. He led three other marshals two men and one woman. They all wore green jump suits with Kevlar vest. They wore side arms with leg straps.

"Carlton Mack, Rae Van Lewin and Columbus Hoover." Tobias breezed through introduction. "Last night there was a bus accident. The bus carried several female prisoners that were being returned to Chillicothe. During the incident a couple of the women may have wandered off trying to get help. We are in the process of rounding them up."

"How many?" Wendell asked.

"Not your concern." Tobias answered. We believe they will be headed away from here." Tobias pointed to an area map that had been hung.

The uniform police officers looked around as if Wendell had been slapped. The street cops had great resected for Wendell and did not enjoy anything that remotely looked like disrespect.

"Do we have a list of the names?" Abby asked.

"Again, not your concern." Tobias reaffirmed.

"Why are we having this chickenshit meeting." Nash asked.

"It's a chess game." Detective Lopez, Nash's partner answered. "We have the only good hospital between here and the big cities. If there are hurt bad, they would have to come here before there could do anywhere else."

"I have a question." Abby raised her hand.

"Yes detective." Tobias was clearly announced with the progress of the meeting.

"How often does the marshal service put a group of women with no names into a bus without counting how many of them there are?'

"This was a waste of time." One of the officers yelled from the back of the room.

"I say we do not make this a compete waste of time, I'm going on a donut run." Lavon announced. There was cheering as the room cleared.

Chapter 3

"So, here's the deal, Lavon." Wendell had accompanied Lavon to Aarons lab. Lavon had brought donuts for Aaron and his technician during his donut run. Lavon was interested in keeping in good standing with Aaron the lead technician. Aaron was noted to be hard to get along with. Aaron was a slender young black man who was gay and had an almost theatrical presence. But Aaron new his business and had the total respect of his crew.

"I was going to ask you to be my best man, but there is someone else I have known a lot longer and that has had my back through the hardest of times."

"Wendell, I understand and whoever you choose has my fullest support." Lavon confirmed.

"See that's just what I wanted to her you say. I don't think I will have a best man but a best person. I want Webber to stand beside me."

"So, what's the problem?"

"Are those for us?" Aaron asked as he saw the two approaching.

"They sure are." Lavon assured ready to get back to his conversation with Wendell.

"I guess that means you want to take a look at the US Marshals photos?" Aaron asked.

Lavon and Wendell had not thought of it but felt if there was an offer on the table why not. "Oh, Jesus." Wendell exclaimed as Aaron brought of computer images of the bus incident.

"Jesus is right it looks like someone hit the front of this thing with a lightning bolt." Aaron stated taking a donut. "Any idea who the bodies were?"

Speechless Wendell and Lavon stared at each other. "How many." Lavon was finally able to utter.

"You have to check with Doc but I think they want their own guy to take over. I only get pictures because someone from the state cops wanted me to help calculate the impact. You know a bus traveling forty miles hour gets hit by a .50 Caliber max load armor piercing round." Aaron stopped and took another bite. "You know standard high school algebra."

Chapter 4

"Hey Willie, how's it hanging." Julie Poole walked into Salvatore's Pizza with her two brothers Herb and JoJo, the two that had helped her escape the marshal's bus. Wille Cotton was one of the pizza cooks for Salvatore's and he was the early start up man. He did not notice Julie at first then jumped. JoJo flipped the closed sign over so they would not be disturbed.

"Look Poole I am sorry about the way things turned out." Willie began. Wille was a thin black man in his early sixties with dark features.

"No sweat. You did what you had to do. Someone set me up and I was wondering if you had any idea who."

Herb and JoJo stood looking ready for action having a good time watching Willie squirm.

"Willie, do you remember what I said before they sentenced me?" Julie asked.

"I don't want no trouble."

"No what I said was that I am innocent and if you bastards convict me, I am going to come back here and kill ever last one of you if I must do it from my grave. Lucky for me I don't have to do it from the grave. But unlucky for you cause you got to die."

Chapter 5

Lavon and Abby arrived at Salvatore's as requested by Nash and Lopez. The call had come in as a blind call, so they were not informed why they were requested. "They probably want some ideas about what to do for Wendell bachelor's party. And they don't want to use official channels." Lavon guessed.

"I don't care what you clowns do. Beside Wendell hates me. His partner hates me. And before long his new wife will hate me." Abby pouted.

Entering the restaurant, it was clear the place was closed. There was a team of police technicians standing around as if they were waiting for Lavon and Abby to arrive. Lavon and Abby assessed this was not a good sign.

"What up guys." Lavon asked noting the grim look on Nash's face and the equally somber look on Lopez.

"So, in all you experience as a detective have you ever hand to get a body out of a pizza oven?" Nash asked.

"What?" Lavon and Abby asked in concert.

Nash opened the oven door and there was the face of Willie Cotton, smiling from inside the over. His hand was on the side of his face and the soles of his feet faced outward. His back hand obviously been snapped to contort him into this position. One had to wonder if he was dead before he was snapped in half. If he was dead before he was shoved into the oven or if he was dead before the heat was turned on.

9

Lavon's cell phone rang. "Hey, Lavon, this is Noreen, are you busy?" Noreen Tyler is one of Lavon's Seven sisters.

"A little." He answered.

"I just got assigned my first case as an intern. It's a murder case."

The medical examiner arrived, and he begun mumbling a cussing under his breathe about something about the end of humanity as soon has he investigated the oven.

"I sure you will do great honey. How can I help?" Lavon asked.

"Well, it's a murder case."

"Noreen, I guess I am having trouble focusing. See I am looking at a man in a pizza oven and it almost sounded like you said you are on a murder case."

"I did. Maybe I should call you later and you can tell me how the man got into the oven." Noreen hung up.

"I don't care how you do it get him the fuck out of there." The medical examiner grumbled.

LAVON AND ABBY WERE almost back at the police station when they received a call from dispatch asking them to meet the sergeant in charge at the Ameren Electric Office building downtown. No sooner then they arrived they noticed the large crowed out front. The was a tarp over what could only have been a body. Sargent Rush was the sergeant in charge. Sargent Rush was often responsible for training many new sergeants and their transition to their new responsibilities.

"What you got Sargent. A jumper?" Abby asked stepping from the car.

"Judging by where she landed and the distance from the railing. She was fifteen feet into the air and twelve feet out before she stated her descent. So, unless you find a trampoline in the room no."

"You are saying unofficially she was pushed." Lavon asked.

"I am saying unofficially she was hurled. Good luck."

Lavon stool looking up at the place where the woman would have descended. "You know how happy I said I was not to be the primary on the pizza oven case. This doesn't look like any more fun than that."

Lavon and Abby spent most of the rest of the day investigating the death of the woman. She was Barbara Rushmore a ninety-pound woman who as in her mid-thirties. She was a home maker with surprisingly few accomplishments. Her husband said she had no enemies and fewer friends.

Chapter 6

"US Marshals! Come out with your hands up!" Marshal Columbus Hoover yelled to the old frame house. The tracking dogs and lead the Marshals and a team of county police to a small frame house that double as the workshop for small engine repairman and his wife.

"Wait a minute, I want to make a deal." Jolene Hyden yelled back to Hoover. Jolene and Lindsey Burns had met up and hand ran as fast as they could, but their trail was too easy for the dogs to smell together. The dogs were on them hounding them relentlessly. They and came on the small house and with the hopes calling someone the drive them away from the area.

"No deals. We got three dead, what kind of deal did they get." Rae yelled.

"That's just it that shit was just as much a surprise to us as it was to them. All we want is for you bastards not to add time to the time we already got. I had a shot at getting out in a couple of years." Lindsey screamed.

"No deals." Hoover repeated.

"Then fuck all of you." Lindsey screamed back. There as a momentary silence then Jolene screamed a blood curdling scream. You could also hear the cries of the repairman and his wife. "Somebody, get a doctor she stabbed herself." The marshals and the county cops stormed the home. They found Jolene crying holding the twitching body of Lindsey. "Couldn't you have at least lied to her." The repairman's wife asked as she watched the life drain out of Lindsey.

LAVON STRADDLED LYNNS body as she lye seminude in the bed. Lavon was giving her a massage. Lynn Masterson enjoyed having Lavon live with her in her semi mansion. She is a judge. Lynn and Lavon have a new blossoming relationship and the evenings together prove to be some of the best times they can spend. Lavon is about six two and played football for Florida State. He also boxed golden gloves as did many of his six brothers. "Honey, why would a law firm put an intern on a murder case?" Lavon a finally asked.

"My guess is that a chain is only as strong as its weakest link. So, if a lawyer has an interest in business law, they will reenforce her skills in other areas first to be sure she doesn't look like a clown the first time her chosen discipline dips into another area."

"So, it's not like hazing?"

"No." Lynn giggled partially from the area Lavon was massaging and partially from his question. "It's not the military or frat week in college. It's a multimillion-dollar business and I will let you in on a little judge's secret."

Lavon rolled her over and began massaging her top.

"No judge in his right mind is going to let an intern near his court room. Too many ways the decision can be overturned. So, give Noreen all the support you can."

"She doesn't want support for the case she wants support for when daddy finds out."

"Oh. And how did someone get a man into a pizza oven?"

"Sorry as per our agreement I cannot discuss an open case with you Judge." Lavon smugly commented while massaging her to an almost feline purr.

"You don't know either."

"Not a clue."

Chapter 7

"You know team I really like all the reports coming in but there is one type of report I would like to see that seems to be missing." Lt. Dana Crawford began. "How about for shits and grins we get a few arrest reports going. What do you guys think we are cops lets arrest somebody."

"We were going to arrest the husband of the woman that was thrown off that building, but the guy has emphysema and COPD and he can barely breath let alone throw someone through the air." Lavon explained.

"And boss we were going to arrest Cottons wife for putting him in the oven, but she is four foot nine and three hundred fifty pounds. I don't think she could raise her arms that high with nothing in them let alone a human man." Lopez answered.

"Well, I hear from the county cops the US Marshals are at work they got two of the women they were looking for one dead one alive." Crawford announced.

"In hate to be the skeptic in the bunch but I will save my cheering when for when we know the number we started with. Is it two out of three or two out of fifty?"

Chapter 8

Riley Jinkins stood outside his home packing up his truck as he did most mornings. Riley works construction and had a small home repair business of his own on the side.

"Good morning, JoJo. When does that crazy sister of yours get out." Riley saw JoJo appear from behind him. Riley had allowed JoJo to work some small jobs with him since the trial that sent his sister Julia Poole to prison.

"Sooner than you think." JoJo responded as Herb and Julia walked up.

"No way you got parole that fast you must have escaped." Riley's voice no wavering.

"What happen? Did they threaten you. Did you get paid? Just tell me what my butt was worth, mister businessman." Julia gave Riley a contemptuous look.

"You know I hire a shit load of cons and they all sing one song or the other. I was framed or I came from a bad environment. It's all a load of bullshit. You were convicted based on the evidence that was presented. If anybody knew anything different no one brought it into the court room and no one talked to us about it. So, take your medicine like a big bitch and grow up."

"Nice nail gun." Herb and reached into the back of Riley's pick up. "How exactly does something like this work?"

"You freaks don't scare me now put that down."

"I'll show you." JoJo took the nail gun from his brother and shot Riley in the forehead with a nail. Julia took the nail gun from her brother's hand and continued firing the nails into Riley, she then reloaded and fired more.

"WHAT DOES THIS REMIND you of?" Abby asked as she and Lavon examined the nail ridden body of Riley. Wendell had been called as the Sargent on duty and was controlling the crowd and maintaining anyone that might be a witness. When he made the call to the house, he was hoping anyone, but Lavon and Abby answered. Abby and Wendell were on bad terms, and he did not want to deal with it.

"Porcupine right. It looks like human porcupine." Abby answered her own question.

"Abby that is sick even for you." Wendell stated.

"Gee Wendell don't you have some rules to write or something,"

Wendell looked at Abby then at Lavon and chose not to engage and started walking back to the other work that needed to be done.

"Wait a minute. This is not going to work. Wendell is one of the best officers I have ever worked with and the two of you having personal feeling toward each other needs to stop right here and right now. I got somebody killing people. Butcher, bakers, and candlestick makers, in other words normal folks. Not gangsters who may have deserved it. Not gang bangers in drive byes but the very folks we swore to protect and serve." Abby and Wendell could see that Lavon was getting angry.

"Truce." Abby held out her hand.

"Truce." Wendell excepted her handshake.

"You have a point though. These people that have died recently have been the most plan boring people you can think of. Even investigating them puts you to sleep. Makes me almost wish that mess with the Marshals came our way rather than going the other way." Abby noted

Chapter 9

"Ten bucks say I get the first confirmed sale of the day." Car salesman Bart Lowenstein offered to his fellow salesmen as the stood evening the Dodd Motors car lot. "Bet they all confirmed." Herb walked up and pointed to Bart. "Hey, I got just got money from a work comp case and I don't want to blow it so I want to start by buying a new car can you so me something in a compact.?"

"Yeah, I can but a guy your size might feel better in something with a little more room not to mentions a little more zip under the hood." Bart suggested.

"You're probably right but let's start with a test drive on the Yaris."

"Sure, let me photo your driver's license and we can take it for a spin." Bart returned shortly handing Herb back the fake driver license. Herb drove the car off the lot and stopped in back. JoJo and Julia squeezed into the car. Bart pulled down the driver's side vanity mirror and the only thing he could see behind him was the angry eves of Julia. He knew those eyes from weeks during the trial she had stared the same inhuman look at him and the rest of the jury.

"We are going to have such a good time." JoJo slapped the shoulder of Bart. Bart begun mutter a prayer he had been taught as a child by his grandmother, the prayer was about the will of God and our acceptance of the end, when it is at hand. Bart knew for him the end was at hand.

"HEY, BRING THAT YARIS up for a wash it has been out on a test drive." The maintenance supervisor yelled to his crew of young kids trained to keep the cars looking spotless. "Someone pop the trunk and be sure it is clean. One of the kids pop the trunk and the kid closest screamed. The maintenance supervisor walked back to the trunk to see Bart folded and bloody in the trunk on top of the spare. "Somebody, please call the cops, Jesus H Christ."

Chapter 10

Paula Conte ran as fast as she could. it seemed to her like she had been running for two days straight. There had been helicopters to avoid in daylight hours. Dogs to evaded at night and police patrols to elude day and night. She had slide and fallen so many times she had lost count. The neon orange jump suite he wore barely resembled the way it looked when it was issued. It was now covered in grass stains, mud and blood. The paper-thin prison issued shoes she wore were not meant for walking let alone running. She as scared and hungry. She wanted to give up but that was more dangerous for her than running in the dark. Paula heard the rush of water there was a stream. Paula ran to the stream for water to drink and to wash the cuts on her legs.

"Freeze don't move." A man shouted.

Paula threw up her hands.

"Oh, please god don't shoot me." Paula seemed to have lost her last resolve. She burst into tears. "Maybe you should shoot me and get it over with."

He held the riffle down.

"Look lady I stopped pointing the gun at you please stop crying." The man walked a little closer and Paula could see he was about her age.

"Why are you out here anyway this my land my folks left it to me. My name is Todd."

"Well Todd you might want to go ahead and shoot me anyway. I am an escaped prisoner from the women's prison."

"Really. How did you escape."

Paula sat on a rock to rest her feet and continued to nurse her cuts.

"I really didn't some jack ass shot up the bus we were on with something that sounded like a rocket launcher."

"And you took off running?"

"Wouldn't you?"

Paula's stomach made a load growl and she tried to ignore it.

"Well if someone is coming to drag you back there aint no reason you can't eat first. The house is over there." Todd had an old tired looking hound dog following him how didn't seem very interested in much. They started off for the house and Todd noticed Paula was limping he put his arm around her and helped her navigate the short distance.

Inside the small home Paula tore into some cold fried chicken and drank sweet tea like she had not eaten in years.

"Mind if I as you what you did to get locked up."

"Todd you been nice to me so I will tell you the truth. I accepted a blind date."

Todd started laughing.

"Glade to see you find my misery so funny."

"There aint no law that says you can't take a blind date."

"Then Mr. Todd let me tell you." She stopped eating for a moment. "My cousin set me up on a blind date with some guy who wanted to look cool. He thought, hey let's rob a gas station. He drove into the gas station pulls out a gun and some guy walked out of the john and startles him, and he shoots the guy dead as a plank."

"Wow really." Todd's mouth hung open.

"Damn fool didn't get us two blocks before the local sheriff arrested us and made us look like the second coming of Bonnie and Clyde in the news. Next thing I know fat girls are punching me in the face and taking me lunch. I had to lie to my cell mates about why I am locked up, so I don't sound so pathetic."

There was the sound of a dog barking outside close to the house. Paula jumped with a look of total terror on her face.

"That's Blue my hound. He likes people so you didn't hear him when we can up, but he doesn't do well with other dogs. Someone is coming and they have dogs with them."

"Oh shit. Todd, give me a knife and leave the room."

"If the sheriff and the police are coming you can't fight them off with a knife."

"I'm not fighting anymore and I aint going to die little by little. If the catch me, they will put me in a place twice as hard for twice as long. Maybe this is as good a time to end this fucked up life as any."

"Wait a minute. You think you have a pathic existence. I came up here to live with my bride and start a family. She meets some slick talking city boy and she is gone without a single word." Todd walked over to the closet and opened it. "Pathic is the fact that she didn't even take her clothes I have hauled them out a dozen times I even put lighter fluid on them once, but I couldn't put the match to them. I wash them and put them back praying every night she will show up at the door." Todd sank into a chair. "How can a woman get out of a man's bed that loves her and not look back." The sound of the dog pack got louder, and the terror retuned to Paula's face. "Get in the bathroom we will discuss it later." Todd told Paula.

"US Marshals." Tobias called as he approached the porch.

"Welcome Marshal my dog is jealous and has bad manner can you pull back your dog's so they don't hurt him he is old and set in his ways."

"I can certainly relate." Tobias comment brought a round of chuckles from the group

"Do you live here alone son." Tobias asked.

"No it's basically a honeymoon cabin it's me and the little lady."

"Can we come in?" Rae asked walking toward the door not really expecting an answer. The Marshals began casually searching the house.

"Have you seen or heard anything unusual tonight?" Tobias asked.

"Yes, earlier I thought I heard someone down the stream but when I got there, they were gone." Tobias and Rae stared at each other.

"That is where the dog was raising hell." Rae said. "May we see your wife?" Tobias asked. "No offense but could the female marshal look alone. I mean I don't know how they do things where you come from but like I said this is a honeymoon cabin and I don't know what state of dress she might be in."

"Alright guys I got this back up." Rae instructed the male members of the officers. Rae unsnapped the snap on her holster that held down her gun and rested on hand over the handle. She opened the door slightly and Paula had a head full up lather. She was shampooing her hair with her head down toward the sink.

"Come on baby I told you give me a minute for some maintenance, and we can get busy again in just a minute. I don't mind swallowing it but try not to get the stuff in my hair. It is sticky and hard to come out." Paula called without raising her head from the sink. Rae closed the door and walked toward Tobias with a big grin. There was scratching on one of the radios.

"Team two we got some movement on the southside of the stream." "Damn that must be where she came out. Sorry to have bothered you sir." Tobias announced.

"Go her tiger." Rae comments slapping Todd on the arm as she and the armed officers left the cabin.

"TODD, DO YOU THINK you could learn to love me the way you loved that woman that wandered off?" Paula settled on the bed sitting beside Todd in her wet disguise.

"Would you promise not to run off with the first pretty boy you, see?"

"Well there is one way for you to be sure."

"How is that?"

"Give me babies. Lots and lots of babies." She answered.

"You will have to change your name and you won't be able to go to town for a while."

"Todd."

"Yes."

"That girl that left was a damn fool and if she ever finds her way back here, I am going to run her off. Now let's get stated on the baby making thing I don't know about your but its be years for me."

Chapter 11

"I got to stop look at me I am swelling and covered in spots." Olga cried out in the night to Roshanda. Roshanda and Olga and met while escaping and now were trying to work together to escape the area. Olga was a heavy-set white girl with European features and no real physical fitness standards. Rohandra was a muscular black woman that had been raised in East St Louis and had a violent history both inside and outside of confinement.

"You have been slowing me down for miles. That helicopter spotted us, and it won't be long before a patrol shows up you have to keep moving." Roshanda informed.

"I can't run anymore. I can't even breath. I am going to wait here and give myself up."

"Give me your money?'

"What?"

"Those guys gave us all five hundred dollars if you are going to give yourself up you don't need the money. It will get me twice as far."

"Rakshanda, why don't we both give up and when we tell the same story they will know we didn't have anything to do with murdering those marshals."

"There are two thing I know, and one is that US Marshals are obsessed when it comes to tracking down runaways and two is that they kill when they think one of their own was murdered. So, give me your money and you take your chances."

"No, you do what you think you have to." Those might have been the worst words Olga could have spoken because Roshanda hit her in the head with a rock took Olga's money and ran off at what looked like an Olympic speed. Olga was still alive when Marshal Hoover arrived with a group of state police. Hoover radioed for the team being led by Tobias and Rae and the groups converged to assess their progress.

Chapter 12

Lavon and Wendell enter the squad room. They had gotten an early exercise session getting ready for the police vs the fireman charity boxing event. When they approached Lavon's desk, they noticed the small Hispanic news reported, Vinita Gonzalez seated in the guest chair besides Lavon's desk. Abby sat at her desk near Lavon's desk ignoring the reporter. "Lavon, I think we need to call maintenance they need to spray. Some cockroaches are starting to drift into this brand-new building." Abby said looking at Vinita.

"If that's your way of saying you are experiencing some vaginal itching maybe its crabs not cockroaches that are the problem."

"See that Wendell no matter how bad men can joke about each other in a gym women seem to find an even lower level to descend to." Wendell smiled surely waiting for and exit.

"Detective Tyler I understand that Lt Crawford is up for promotion, any comment."

"Just one. Ask her she is less than fifteen feet away."

"I thought given the close relationship between her and your father."

"Okay I'm out of here." Wendell announced was off in a shot.

"Vinita what do you really want? I mean nobody cares about a forty-year-old romance that may or may not have happened. I don't even think my momma would like to hear about them slopping around in the mud at Woodstock, if in fact that is what happen. You'll put your viewers to sleep."

"What is up with the multiple murders? Give me the inside scoop. And we can play as nice as you please."

"What we need is a really good vice squad." Abby mumbled.

"I tell you what right now the murders are being handled as separate events if we find a connection, we will call you first."

"Then I can look forward to a visit from the organ grinder without his monkey." She got up and sashayed away.

"Abby, you got a minute?" Lavon asked after the reporter was gone.

"Why you need me to help you grind your organs I thought that was Lynns job."

"I need you to look at that map the Marshals showed us the other day. They got another runner according to Wendell and the street cops."

IN FRONT OF THE MAP Abby and Lavon examined the points where Olga was found and where the standoff took place. "There is something wrong here and I am not sure what?" Lavon stared staring at the map.

"Well it's like they said everyone is headed away from Shepard's pass. Beside we have enough to do here we don't have to worry about those clowns."

Chapter 13

M organ Norton had just completed her work out. She had a small gym in her garage she used as a dojo. She was a second-degree black belt and used the dojo in her home to practice without interruption. The door to the garage raised and Julia Poole stood there with her brothers. Julia was a lean deceptively strong woman who fought in mixed martial arts and ultimate fighting before her sentencing and incarceration. Julia was dressed in a pair of sweatpants and a tee shirt with her hair in a ponytail. "I know who you are. Maybe I should call the police." Morgan stated blandly to Julia ignoring her brothers.

"You could do that but that belt you are wearing is more than a piece of cloth. It's the symbol of honesty and integrity. It's a symbol of all they have worn it and worked hard to achieve it, so you will give me a minute."

Morgan smiled and nodded.

"A long time ago a sensei told me that there are two ways to earn a black belt. One is to train for years and one day one will be granted. The other is to take one off the waist fairly from someone you though were wearing it and did not deserve it."

"So that's why you are here for me to kick your ass. And you brought your brothers to what, referee."

"No, they came so no one could interfere. No referees no clock no rules."

"Then shall we begin."

Before the light windbreaker Julia was wearing could hit the floor the fight was in full effect. Morgan's arsenal was filled with a merciless round house kicks followed by a devastating spinning back kick. Morgan unloaded with a serious of front snap kicks that were smothered by Julia, had they not they would have lifted her off the floor. One of the main issues with self-defense is that it is defense. Most of Morgan's training was defensive and Julia knew it. Morgan's offensive arsenal was lacking. Offensive assault is taught in warrior or kill or be killed training. The kind you get fighting in prison fighting for your life. No sooner than Julia detected that Morgan had drained some of the energy she possessed Julia shot a spinning back hand to Morgan's face then grabbed her wrist and stepped under to twist the wrist. When Morgan tried to step out of the arm bar her back was exposed, and Julia put her left arm around Morgan's windpipe locking it with her right fist. Julia then jumped up and wrapped her legs in a scissor around Morgan from behind and squeezed her. Moran was now being choked and her ribs being crushed at the same time. Morgan tried to tap out, but it was useless, Paula had no desire nor capacity for mercy. There was a crunching sound and death speeded toward Moran like a freight train in the night and carried her off. Julia removed Morgan's belt and her brothers applauded and helped he put her jacket back on. "See boys that is how it's done. If they had not messed up my life, I would have had the title." Julia swung he fist into the air in victory.

Chapter 14

"Stop US Marshal Service." Carlton Mack yelled at the running woman.

"Call off the dog I have a phobia you can't torcher me it's in the constitution." Karlene Wilson screamed back over her shoulders as she found for to put distance between herself and the gaining dogs.

The crowd of cops raced toward Karlene. "Stop or I will shoot." One of the deputies yelled.

Karlene had stopped with her back to a cliff that led to the highway beneath. The dog still approached her. "Please call them back. I give up." One of the dogs raced toward her snarling.

"No." Carlton Mack screamed and Karlene thew herself into the precipitate below. She landed in a pile of jaded rocks below.

"Damn.Damn.Damn." Carlton repeated.

"DO YOU THINK IT WAS two attackers?" Nash asked. Detective Nash was kneeling with the medical examiner in front of the body of Morgan.

"One attacker." Lavon answered walking up.

"How do you figure the woman was a black belt instructor." Nash questioned. The Medial examiner waited for Lavon's explanation.

"She was choked in a rear naked choak with leg scissors around her waist. Those marks are from the knees of the attacker. Probably a woman or a teenage boy judging by the approximate length of the humorous based on where the knees would intersect."

"Bravo Mr. Tyler it shows you never fell asleep in your anatomy classes at the academy." The medical examiner applauded.

"You want to rock paper scissors for this case or what?" Lopez asked.

Chapter 15

"Hey, Chester, how's it hanging." Julia approached Chester Rinehart as he walked from the drugs store headed back to his car. Chester was the public defender that oversaw Julia's case before her conviction. Chester stopped and swallowed he tried not to look at his car on the parking lot where his daughter sat watching him returning to the car. He and promised to sneak her a piece of chocolate candy and not let her mother know. "You are looking really good these days." "Look Julia I don't have any idea how you got here but..."

"No, you don't because you sold my ass for forty pieces of silver. Now at least tell me it was worth it."

Terror overtook Chester's eyes there was an end coming who all was included was his only thought.

"Okay so I cut a deal they said you did it. No big deal."

"No big deal. You ended my life. You lost me my career as a fighter." Julia basked in the raw fear that emanated from his eyes for a moment before stabbing in the throat with a sharp knife he never saw coming. Someone was coming from the store. Julia and her brothers walked casually away.

Before Lavon and Nash could decide who had the karate killing case the dispatcher called Lavon and Abby to report to the drugstore for a murder with meant the karate kill went to Lopez and Nash.

"THE GUY IS RINEHART. A public defender I knew him." Webber told Lavon trying to ignore Abby. A little girl worked her way through the crowd and took Lavon by the hand.

"He was my father I saw her kill him." Lavon kneeled and waited. "It was a She-devil." Webber knelled beside them.

"How do you know it was a she-devil." Weber asked to the amazement of Lavon that the statement made sense to Webber.

"She was tagged." The girl was about nine or ten and spoke in clear factual tone, something the child of an attorney may have learned long before some other children.

The little girl was Megan Reinhart and one of the local high school teams has the Sundevil as a mascot. Some of the female teams use the She devil as their calling card. When they when the championships or any league title they tag themselves by tattooing the she-devils on their wrist. Webber explained this to Lavon and Abby. Webber as a street cop had been involved in youth programs and was well aware of the symbol. Abby knew a social worker named Chapman and had Chapman join Lavon herself and Megan for a trip to the High school.

"I AM SORRY WE HAVE the interest of the students to protect so without a warrant stating sufficient cause we can't assist you in questions on students past or present." Mrs. Vincent the high school vice principal informed Lavon. They spoke in the hallway outside her office. There was trophy cased of winning school teams and group pictures of the winning team for various sports.

"There she is that's the woman the killed my father." Megan was pointing at a woman in a past group photo. "There she is again in this picture too." Megan moved down a little. Her hair is different in this one but there she is." Lavon looked at the picture in the case. Megan hand pointed out the same girl in each of the photos she had pointed to. It was a women's wrestling team for three different years.

"I don't know about you but that's the best unsolicited line up pick I have ever even heard about." Abby stated.

"Julia Poole." Lavon read from the small names printed below.

"Oh god not that one." Mrs. Vincent exclaimed.

"Care to share with the class Mrs. Vincent." Abby requested.

"She is not a student. He was at some point. Best female wrestler the Midwest has ever seen. She and those brother of hers were a nightmare."

LAVON, MEGAN AND CHAPMAN sat eating hamburgers at Lavon's desk and the clerk walked up.

"I like a good joke as much as the next girl, but I really am business." Lavon surveyed his fellow diners, but they also had no clue as to what the issue was.

"Okay what did I do wrong?" Lavon asked.

"You wanted a current address on Julia Poole."

"Right."

"She is in prison at Chillicothe." Abby and Lavon stared at each other for a moment. Bombarded not by the same thoughts.

ABBY, LAVON, NASH, Lopez, and Aaron collected in one of the meeting rooms. "I want to be the first to say this covert stuff is not my usual thing." Aaron announced.

"Duly noted. "Lavon responded.

"What is so hush hush?" Nash asked.

"We think we have a make on the killers."

"And it's a secret?" Aaron asked.

"We may find ourselves in a war with the US Marshals." Lavon explained.

"I hope you are talking softball teams or Texas holdem. Because there is a lot less of you than there is of them." Aaron quivered.

"Let's look at what we know. First, we have a meeting telling us there was a traffic accident involving a Marshals van." Lavon looked at Aaron. "Please show the pictures of that accident."

"Holy glory." Nash exclaimed.

"It looks like they were shot at with howitzers." Lopez verified. "But this still looks like a problem for the Marshals to clean up."

"Maybe but look closely the shooter were shooting for the cab where the marshals are. Not shooting at the body of the bus. That smells like jail break." Abby noted.

"We got an ID on the killer for the public defender." Lavon moved on.

"Dissatisfied customer. Julia Poole, only her address says she is in Chillicothe women's prison. We called Chillicothe and they say she is registered there but they cannot confirm her presence." Abby noted.

"See the thing that was bothering me this morning about the map of where the runners are being found is that they should be sprawled all over the place like people running from a fire." Lavon put the map on the table. "They are not they are being led away from Shepherd's Pass."

"You are saying who ever busted someone out of the marshals bus wanted to lead the marshals on a merry chase while they had time to do dirt in Shepherds Pass." Nash noted. "And why don't we sound the alarm."

Aaron raised his hand. "I vote sound the alarm."

"The problem with that is it is the marshal's problem so first we must convince them that it is their problem. Then we wait until they swing into action."

"I see your point. We got mom and pops dropping dead all over town." Lopez commented. "Their job with be to capture Julia and they don't really have to care how many normal voters get wasted in the process.

"So, Lavon what's the alternative?" Nash asked.

"Well, she took out her public defender. I will bet a month's pay that everyone that had died recently was on her jury. Just common folks trying to do their civic duty." Lavon added.

"So we get the list of jurors and the judge and prosecutor. We have uniforms label these as high value targets and with stay in communication. Remember this group folded a man up and stuck him in an oven and the smallest one of the team is a woman how beat a black belt to death." Abby added.

"Good thing you we got you the designated shooter on board." Lopez stated.

"That's offensive, but I am going to let it slide this time." Abby's choice of statement caused Lavon to smile.

"So, the next move is to find out who needs special protection and slowly bring uniform cops into service to help. Then we get out a description of the bad people and no one approaches alone."

THE COLLECTING OF INFORMATION went much quicker now that Lavon's team knew not only what they were looking for but who they had to avoid. It even helped Lavon come up with a plan to slow down the killings. This plan involved Vinita the news reporter.

"I believe we have a person of interest that may be responsible for the killings, but we would like your help." Lavon sat across from Vinita Gonzalez. She wore provocative clothing and heavy makeup. She drew great pleasure in using flirtation to disarm people for her interviews. "How do I know you are not trying to pimp me."

"Because I feel someone gave an order for all cops to stonewall the news and it's hurting both sides. If you don't want to be the one to take a chance, I can talk to someone else. I just thought since you came to me first, I should respect that." Lavon lied knowing he did not know anyone else he could use to help with this part of the plan.

She batted her eyelashes and leaned forward to give Lavon a good view of her cleavage. "Okay so say I am listening."

"We have a person of interest his name is JoJo Poole. He is a local thug with a low IQ."

"And what makes you think he is involved in the killings."

"The Public Defender that was killed represented his sister and lost and he feels the case was fixed."

"Wow." She squealed. "This is the kind of stuff we need to lead the news."

"Now you must keep it confidential how you got the tip. And what I will do is I will try to let you know when we find him and plan to arrest."

"Detective Tyler I would have your baby for less."

"Why don't we do this together first."

"Sure, your choice."

"JOJO POOLE. THIS IS the Shepherds Pass police put your hands up." Officer Webber called. The police had received a call that JoJo was spotted shortly after the news program ran on the tv. JoJo stepped out of a rundown motel room in the lower 9 blocks of Shepard's Pass were drugs and prostitution are prevalent. He had availed himself of the services of a lady of the evening and was on his way to his car. Weber stood with her gun pointed at JoJo she had an officer she did not know and could not recognize backing her up. "Sir you are wanted for questioning in multiple homicides do you understand?"

"Fuck you Bitch." JoJo yelled. Webber could remember being shot before and she knew a second's hesitation could cost her life. She also knew the news reporter was somewhere hiding with a camera crew.

"Sir we need to talk."

"Talk to this." JoJo pulled a gun from the small of his back and before he could fire Webber fired a round of shots center mass and he flew backward. The unknown officer stood there frozen. "Hey, you go in there and clear that room, now." Webber knew to clear the area when they might be looking for multiple suspects.

Vinita ran up to Webber. "Wow I keep hanging out with you guys that could be my ticket out of this one-horse town."

"Lady give it a rest."

"All clear." the other officer call back.

Chapter 16

Lt Crawford sat on the edge of her desk looking from Lavon to Abby to Nash then to Lopez, then back again. "We can explain." Nash began.

"No detective Nash please don't. This is my first mutiny and I want to enjoy it. Besides this isn't your office just yet." She rubbed he hands together. "That is right I am taking the position upstairs and command feels Nash is ready to take my spot here. So, my I ask, are covert operations going to become standard?" Lopez stood and slowly went over the meeting that led to the discover that the marshals has left out information that would have helped their investigation. She then explained how the killers had been identified.

"So, somewhere in here is some good police work?" Crawford concluded. "Has this group planned any further secret missions to get the other killers or are you keeping that secret from me as well." Crawford looked directly at Lavon.

"It's not a secret it's just that we haven't come up with it. This part of the plan was to stop them from going down the list killing normal folks." Addy looked at Crawford. "Voters serve on juries. The mayor wants to be seen as protecting the lives of voters. Beside no one is going to serve on a jury it they know that means a death sentence."

"Alright you clowns have convinced me now find those other two nut cases before the marshals figure out what's up and show up tearing the place apart looking for Julia Poole. Remember they have broad far-reaching powers and even the mayor is limited in what he can do to slow them down when they get in a rush. Also, remember they have lost over 200 officers in the line of duty since the sixties they will not play with Poole, so you don't either."

"Looks like you are going to be looking for someone new to ride with." Lavon mentioned to detective Lopez.

"You can't have Lavon we have a kid together his name is Cletus." Abby told Lopez. Lopez looked at Lavon in shock.

"Cletus is her dog."

"Lopez laughed. "No one would be cruel enough to name a dog Cletus."

"I HEAR YOU GOT YOUR first kill tonight." Lavon met Webber at Patrick's, a bar facing the man-made lake in Shepard's Pass. Patrick's is often the stop off place for police and hospital personal after a long shift.

"Yeah. Well maybe it will hit me later, but I don't feel bad."

"Could it be that you were shot yourself recently and that was a reminder that it is not a game."

Webber smiled. "I hand not thought about it that way but being shot myself did enter my mind. I was also worried about the rookie and him possibly freezing and getting shot. I guess that is why Wendell has always been so protective of me."

"Wendell is protective of you because you two share an undefined love."

"What's that?'

"Well it's not romantic love it's more like brother and sister or mentor and student." Webber drank more of her beer. "If you want the best man job I will understand."

"No, I want you to do it. Its best person and you are one of the best persons I know. How does your wife feel about it. She is all there for me."

"Does she know she is going to lose her ass if she bets against me and Wendell in the boxing matches."

"She says she saw you fight Lucas, and no one is going to stop you, but she says they have a guy to take out Wendell."

"Then I guess I had better go home and plan more strategy for Wendell. You know Wendell and Abby have agreed to stop fighting for the time being. I hope you will consider it also. I would hate to see you damage your career in a tiff with my silly partner."

As Lavon was leaving Webber stopped him. "Does Lynn know how special you are?"

"She does and does your wife know what a wonderful person you are?"

Chapter 17

"Okay let's straighten this out one last time." Terrell stated. Terrell was the head of the bailiffs for the courts building. He oversaw the protection of the judges and was frequently referred to as their babysitter. He had met Judge Wakefield's SUV as the judge drove into the underground parking. Terrell assisted him from the vehicle. "How much did you weigh in college?" Terrell asked the judge. "About 190 in my prime, why." Terrell shook his head. "Were getting there. Now how much do you weigh?" The judge looked away the way bad liars do. "About 175." Terrell smiled. "More like one sixty."

"No fair you law enforcement types see height and weight in your sleep."

The men strolled toward the elevators, but Terrell noticed two figures near a van. They were in police uniforms. One was a large man not quite as large as Terrell. Terrell was three hundred twenty and had played football as a nose tackle. The man in police uniform was large but not as solid. the officer with him was a woman with her hair in a ponytail. Terrell had gotten a notice that increase security may be need for the judge and had gone to the garage to escort him personally. Terrell thought maybe the cops sent some extra help.

"The point is you still use the same hard rubber sixteen-pound ball you used back in college. It's time for you to switch to a fourteen-pound composite." The judge made a look like a child getting an unwanted plate of Brussels sprots.

"Look you go into full back swing and the ball weight is causing you to drift off just a little and it's giving your table leg splits every other frame."

"So, I adjust to compensate."

"In bowling one shoe has the slide on the bottom and the other the break. You are already sliding off course when the ball leaves your hand." There was a clunking sound like something heavy metal was unloaded from the van.

"Down." Terrell screamed grabbing the Judge and pulling him like a rag doll toward one off the concrete columns in the garage. There was as swoosh and a huge explosion as the concrete column burst and concrete dust filled the air. The garage floor shook. A chuck of the column was now missing, and the rebar showed. Car alarms all over the garage sounded and lights flashed. Swoosh the second rocket like shot blasted and more concrete was liberated into the air. The vibration of the second show blasted out car windows.

"Judge I need you to stay down. I got some work to do." Terrell announced before starting a fast commando craw past some parked cars. And SUV exploded and caught fire as a third .50 caliber armor piercing round shot through a compact car, in one side and out the other setting the SUV in full blaze. A stairway door open and people poured out running stumbling falling and trampling to get out. Terrell used the disarray to get up and run and make a loop to where he had seen the fake officers setting up. Where the .50 caliber fire was coming from. He saw Herb and Julia in their police uniforms. Herb barely had time to look up before being tackled full on by Terrell. Terrell slammed Herb into Paula and she fell stumbling to get up. Two real uniform police showed up confused while a bailiff would be tackling a uniformed cop before they could figure it out Julia shot one of them in the head and the other office had just enough time to duck to avoid a similar fate. She ran for the stairway. Terrell wrestled Herb and cuffed him. The surviving uniformed officer started calling for back up and an ambulance. Terrell put Herb in the custody of the officer and returned to the judge. "One thing you have to remember Judge."

"Yes, Terrell." The judge looked at Terrell expecting great wisdom.

"You have got to keep your thumb toward the pocket during your release."

Chapter 18

"**D**o you think we are going to get a spanking." Abby asked Lavon as she saw Sean Hardcastle the Mayors Public relations man headed toward the office of Lt Crawford. Hardcastle did not make it inside her office as she ran out of her office carrying a bullet proof vest. "Code 911 all officers to the courts building. We are under attack." She yelled. Abby turned and looked at Lavon. "You know I am starting to like this Julia girl."

THE NEW COURTS BUILDING was just across the noll from the new police station but in no time flat there was a huge crowd. Lavon notice Vinita Gonzalez talking to a man in a yellow hard hat. Lavon approached. "Looks like we have Detective Tyler to the rescue once again."

"You the cop in charge?" Yellow hat asked in a strong Brooklyn accent.

"Sure, he is." Vinita confirmed.

"I'm with the city engineer's office Some lame brain shot support columns out of that building. I am declaring the building structurally unsound until further notice it's got to be evacuated."

"Hey Lavon. Your suspect is still in the building." Terrell yelled to Lavon.

"Hey moron, are you actually going in there after her?" Abby asked from behind Lavon. "Yeah, with any luck the building will fall on both of us, and this nightmare will be over."

"In that case I'll be joining you. And don't flatter yourself I just got to meet this bitch."

"HEY COUNTRY BOY WHY is it I think you know where you are going?" Abby asked. The city had cut the main power to the building and the emergency light were on. Lavon and Abby kept running into small pockets of people to afraid to run. They directed the people they encounter to leave using the stair well.

"It's because I know where she is." Abby followed close with her gun drawn. "She is headed for the eighth floor." Abby smiled. "Right makes sense now." The eight floor was where the District Attorney's offices were. Arriving at the eight floor they stopped to take a breath before meeting fate in its most raw form.

"Hey Julia can we talk for a moment before we kill each other." Lavon called into the hallway as he and Abby approached. Lavon and Abby eased down the corridor. There was a dismal feel to the office with the emergency lights flashing.

"Where the fuck you from Country boy?" Finally, Julia yelled back.

"Lamont Mississippi." Lavon answered. "What's there?"

"Nothing much."

"Help me." A woman's voice streaked.

"Well ma'am I don't know if I am here to help you or the help her." There was a silence. "You marshals are full of tricks." Julia finally called out.

"No ma'am I am a Shepherd's Pass cop. That's how I knew what room to find you in."

"Really."

"Yeah really. They screwed you. They sold you down the river as part of a package deal and didn't even look at your case. Probably thought you would be freed on appeal anyway what they did not know is that when a great fighter like you gets locked up everybody wants to kicked your ass. So, they got bragging rights. So, there you are fight after fight. Getting harder and harder and adding time to your time" There was a rustling inside one of the offices. Lavon and Abby had a better idea which office held Julia. "I want to know if you knew it was the prosecutor that made a deal with your public defender why kill all those innocent people?'

"Innocent." Julia was outraged at the notion. "Those innocent basters could have asked questions they could have stalled until they were presented with the truth instead, they were so busy with their own lives. Well, I gave them their own lives up close. That little bastard so in a hurry to put stuff in a pizza oven when I shoved his ass in one. The prick that wanted to go nail some stuff I nailed his ass."

"Please don't let her kill me." A faint woman's voice cried out in terror. Abby had moved to a position that would allow her to see inside the room. Abby stepped out with her gun pointed at Julia. Julia had her butt rested on the desk with her legs wrapped around the waist of district attorney Forrest from behind. Forrest was a small woman of dark complexion. She was not remarkable in beauty nor was she hideous.

She was just as unmarkable as the rest of the victim. Julia had her left arm around the District Attorneys neck and her right hand had a .9 mm pistol. Julia had the pistol pointed at her own head. Lavon stepped out facing Julia and Forrest.

"You know country boy in a different life we could have been good together." In a planned motion Julia swung her body weight and snapped the neck of Forrest while crushing her ribs just prior to shooting herself in the head. The two women lye on the floor looking like a piece of abstract art. One woman normal and plain intertwined with a woman forced into an angry life. Both women covered in the same blood. Then as miraculously as life allows, death Julia seem to revert to that innocent girl that had won all those state wrestling championships years and years in a row.

"I say we find the US Marshals and give them a hard time." Abby suggested.

"Works for me."

Chapter 19

Lavon and Abby sat at their desk. They had been scolded by the US Marshals. Followed by a scolding by Mr. Hardcastle for working with the news media. They began the trek up the treacherous mountain of paperwork that had been created by recent events. A small thin man in a worn suit walked in and sat in Lavon's guest chair.

"Are you Detective Tyler."

"Yes."

"I came here to be arrested."

Lavon and Abby stopped and considered the man.

"What do you think we should arrest you for sir."

"Wentworth." He introduced himself.

"Mr. Wentworth, what crime have you committed?" Abby asked.

"Multiple Murders. And I wont fight you in court."

The confusion on Abby and Lavon's faces registered clearly.

"Who did you kill?" Lavon asked.

"Well let's see. There was the three US Marshals. The jurors. The cop that got shot in the head. And most of all my best friend. Assistant District Attorney Forrest." The man looked like he might pass out at any moment. A great weight had been lifted from his shoulders.

"Sir can you explain. Just for the record." Lavon rested back in his chair.

"I am the one that authorized those speedy motions that got Julia and a bunch of others signed off on a wholesale plea agreement. I made the deal with the Public Defenders that got her locked up. She was so angry and seemed so violent who would have thought she was innocent. All my life I have looked at numbers. Statistics. Metrics. Numbers. I saw a way to save Shepherds Pass a few dollars and I took it." Wentworth stopped for a moment and cleaned the thick glasses wore. Tears were welling up in his eyes. "Did you know Forrest and my children have breakfast together more morning than you can imagine. Now she is dead at my hand."

"Sir we can't lock you up for being cheap. Otherwise, my uncle Elmer would never see the light of day." Lavon stated.

"Sir what I think my partner, Tennessee Ernie Ford is trying to say is that there are number of people that share in the responsibility for letting things get so out of control. The Marshals, the court system and even us to a degree." Abby tried to help explain.

"Mr. Wentworth you now know what the possible outcome is of scrimping in the wrong places when it comes to the justice system. You are inside. Fix it. Please don't create another Julia Poole."

Chapter 20

"The Marshals say they have accounted for eight of the ten girls that escaped from the bus. Some tough black girl named Roshanda and some girl named Paula Conte. They say they think they can track Roshanda through her old haunts, she seems to be a creature of habit. But Paula Conte they say is no real threat to anyone. She might have drowned trying to find a safe place to cross the spring. But anyway, it goes unless one of them shows un in Shepherds Pass it aint my problem." Lavon stated as he polished Lynns toenails. They had spent much of the evening helping Wendell and Nya to plan their wedding and now was some alone time for them. "Is Webber really going to be best man?"

"Its best persons and yes."

"Is everyone alright with that?"

"Well, a lot of the cops Wendell has worked with are female and I think they look at it like a chance not to be left out of the tom foolery. I mean he is having a co-ed bachelor party and that has got to be a lot said for acceptance."

"What about your partner?"

"She is still a pain in the ass, but I don't know if I could have made it through the day today without her." Lavon sat back to admire his work. "Yes, now those look more like a judge's toes should look."

Just as it has been the duty of lighthouses for thousands of years to guide ships safely into harbors. Thank you for allowing us at the Looking Glass Lighthouse to steer your thoughts dreams and imagination safely to a port of enjoyment.

We are pleased that you have chosen to join us on this journey.

Please feel free to send feedback, questions, and comments to Lookingglasslighthouse@gmail.com and be sure to make your preferred literature vendor aware of your experience.

As a special thank you for allowing us to entertain you we would like to give you a special sneak peek into the next episode of Shepherds Pass- Treasure at Shepherds Pass and a look inside Noreen Tyler- A Tyler Girl Adventure

Chapter 1

Treasure at Shepherds Pass

On a warm August day in 1953, four men entered the Roosevelt Federal Bank in St. Louis with the intent of robbing the bank. They made a series of miscalculations that would lead to a trail of dead bodies and set off treasure hunts that would end only generations later. The four men were Erwin Appleton, George Toole, Bolden Tucker, and Melvin Price. Their leader was Erwin Appleton. They had met in the army and had decided to apply their crafts they had learned to one bank job, separate then meet a year later and split the proceeds.

According to the FBI Unified Crime Report, a collection of facts and figures documented by the FBI utilizing a collection of information from all the charted police forces in the United States, the more bank robbers successfully commit a robbery the higher the chances they will be caught. The FBI uses patterns and methods to track bank robbers. One robbery leaves little pattern. Also, according to FBI data if the bank robbers leave with the proceeds from the bank between 22% and 25% is never returned. Elroy Price, Melvin Price's younger brother had been recruited to drive the getaway van. The first item of major consequence of miscalculation was not completely foreseeable. Banks hold a set number of receipts at the bank and send excess amounts of receipts to the Federal Reserve.

Due to a merger, there were excessive amounts held at the bank they entered being prepared to be sent out to the Federal Reserve. This meant that instead of the 200,000 they had estimated they would steal they found themselves standing in front of over 281,000,000.00. Many of the banks involved in the merger had gold double eagle coins and 1000.00 bills that were being taken out of circulation.

The second miscalculation of significant consequence was the large number of guards. These men had never worked together which gave the small team of four trained soldiers who had recently returned from the battlefield a huge advantage leading to the blood bath as guards, of whom had never fired their weapons in close combat lost their lives.

The next consequence involved Erwin Appleton who after hiding the money where only he would know where it was returned home and found his next-door neighbor in his bed having sex with his wife. Appleton took the gun he had just used in multiple homicidal bank robberies and shot his wife and neighbor to death. Appleton was convicted of two counts of murder and put in the penitentiary. Several years into Appleton's stay in the pen the FBI decided to update its database of ballistics and in doing so matched the weapon used in the Roosevelt Federal job to Appleton.

The funds from the Roosevelt job were not recovered when Appleton was charged, and a host of deal-making began.

APPLETON CONVICTED had been for the robbery and the murders and given life in prison. Yet still another unfortunate event shaped the future treasure hunt. In a prison gang rumble, in which Appleton was not involved directly involved; was caught in the middle and sustained severe brain damage. His ability to remember was destroyed.

Noreen Tyler
A Tyler Girl Adventure

Chapter one

B ailey slowing walked across the pool area. It was early fall in St. Louis and the weather was mild. Bailey wore only a towel that she had wrapped around herself. She a carried an open bottle of wine in one hand and a glass in the other. The neighborhood was one of St. Louis's gated places with a private street. It was night and she felt sad. Bailey had just finished making love but it in no way sufficed to cure the aching she felt. She had run the risk of hurting Simon. Bailey looked toward the main house resisting the urge to burst open the back doors that were never locked and throw herself on Simon's mercy. The fight had been her fault she knew it. How could she dare to challenge his love for her. He had filled so many voids that she never thought could never be filled. Even her parents had no comprehension of what Simon meant to her. "Oh, my poor Simon." She thought. "Probably in one of those creative trances. I'll beg your forgiveness in the morning." Bailey walked to the hot tub and dropped her towel. She looked down for a moment admiring her body. She was nineteen and had greater than perfect body. Even women who modeled had the tendency to be mushy in areas. Sports made her firm and strong. She lye back in the hot tub and enjoyed her wine. There was a sound of music coming from the guest house and music started to play louder as the guest house door open.

"Oh, look we don't want to talk about it anymore. It was great but all good things come to an end." Bailey uttered just before being shot three times in the chest. Her eyes opened wide in astonishment. Was she shocked to be leaving life or shocked to be entering into whatever comes next. There was no asking her now.

Chapter 2

"Gee, this Crap is nasty." Doris Fleischman commented making a face the reveal how vile she thought the green energy drink was.

"Mine tastes like toxic waste; it's got to be good for you," Abby responded. The two women had just left a workout session at Galaxy Plus Gym in Shepherds Pass. Doris and Abby had been working out together since they met at the tables of Alcoholics Anonymous.

"Walk with me to my car, Sister." Doris requested.

The parking lot had several cars parked but there were no people present. Doris opened the door of her rusted Nissan and reached for the back seat. She retrieved a small English Bulldog puppy that looked too young to be away from his mother. Doris handed it to Abby who looked shocked.

"What is this?"

"It's a dog."

"Why are you giving me a dog? I don't even know if I like dogs."

"He is a puppy, so I guess the two of you have time to work it out."

"What?"

The puppy opened his eyes and gave Abby a sad stare. He blinked as if having trouble focusing then pushed with his head to nuzzle against Abby.

"Looks like love at first sight to me. Look girl, I owe you money. The chessedick that breeds these puppies owed me money, so he gave me the puppy."

"So, you keep him."

"Can't, they won't allow it in my apartment. You can sell him and make a profit."

Both women rested against the car for the moment enjoying the August breeze. "Does he have a name?"

"Tell me again about the dream you keep having that makes you nervous." Doris seemed to be ignoring Abby's question.

"THERE I WAS IN MY APARTMENT and the country guy I work with walked into the room. He slings me on the bed and rips my clothes off. He screws me every which way possible. No words, nothing. Then he walks out."

"I thought you like men that are basic."

"I don't even know if I like this guy. And I don't think he likes me. But wow it's so real."

While the girls are talking a red Challenger hellcat drives up and two guys are staring at Doris. She knew them.

"How's that ass, Dottie?" A stingy-haired guy with a narrow face and five o'clock shadows asked, eyeing Doris.

"I'm good. Scott." Scott surveyed the area as if trying to see who might be watching.

"Hand me my purse?" Abby requested Doris. Doris reached into the car and reappeared with the purse and handed it to Abby who was under inspection by the two men in the challenger. Abby noticed the strong smell of marijuana at about the same time she noticed the blue van approaching. Abby, being a police detective, did not like the way the van stopped and blocked the Nissan. It was not by accident that the two groups of guys had blocked their departure.

"Is your friend up for the game?" Scott asked Doris.

"No way she's a straight girl and so am I now."

"Fuck that get in the van."

The door to the van slid open and four guys stepped out. They all had handguns in their waistbands. Abby adjusted her position to get a clear field of vision between herself and the group developing. Abby's training as a cop was moving her around as if on autopilot. Something bad was unfolding. No stopping it now. Only minimize the damage. Abby looked back over her shoulder hoping someone was watching.

"Look she doesn't want to go," Abby stated.

"What's the puppy's name?" The oldest man from the van addressed Abby.

"Cletus."

They all laughed.

"Don't laugh at his name you might hurt his feelings."

"Shouldn't he be wearing suspenders or something?"

Eric, the older of the team asked.

"Dottie this bitch is crazier than you are." Scott assessed.

Scott reached into the challenger and pulled out a .357 and pointed it at Dottie. "You know there is only one way for this to end."

At the click of Scott cocking the hammer of the colt python Abby fired and shot Scott in the center of his forehead. This did not however stop Scott's gun from firing and shooting Doris in the head and spaying Abby and Cletus with blood, scull fragments, and what appeared to be brain matter.

"Police," Abby screamed flipping the puppy into the back of the Nissan. One of the crew from the van drew his gun and Abby shot him center mass and he fell backward into the oldest man. Abby looked out of the corner of her eye and found herself staring down the shaky barrel of a gun she spun as her training took over again and she fired. The gun facing her fired the bullet shot slightly past her head as her shot went into the chest of the shooter. She ducked behind a parked car as the driver of the hellcat revved the engine with the demonic howl it manufactures. The other men were piling into the van. Abby jumped up and shot through the out-the-back window of the escaping hellcat as the van took off as well. Abby heard the mournful cry of Doris lying in a pool of her blood. Abby put her finger in Doris's blood and wrote down the last three numbers from the escaping hell cat and the last three from the van.

"Don't cry, Sister. All I want is to die sober. I might get my wish." Doris coughed and expelled blood. A crowd had appeared out of nowhere watching the mayhem.

"One of you motherfuckers dial 911," Abby yelled at the top of her lungs. Abby retrieved Cletus from the car, and he seemed to take it as his job to cheer her up, but this was not completely possible.

Also by Alex Mitchell